Oprah
The Little Speaker

by CAROLE BOSTON WEATHERFORD

illustrated by LONDON LADD

MARSHALL CAVENDISH CHILDREN

FOR ALL GOD'S CHILDREN

—C.B.W.

TO THE PAUL FAMILY; THANK YOU FOR YOUR LOVE AND KINDNESS

—L.L.

Text copyright © 2010 by Carole Boston Weatherford
Illustrations copyright © 2010 by London Ladd
All rights reserved
Marshall Cavendish Corporation, 99 White Plains Road, Tarrytown, NY 10591
www.marshallcavendish.us/kids

Library of Congress Cataloging-in-Publication Data
Weatherford, Carole Boston, 1956-
Oprah : the little speaker / by Carole Boston Weatherford ; illustrated by London Ladd. — 1st ed.
p. cm.
ISBN 978-0-7614-5632-2
1. Winfrey, Oprah—Juvenile literature. 2. Television personalities--United States--Biography--Juvenile literature. 3. Actors—United States—Biography—Juvenile literature. I. Ladd, London. II. Title.
PN1992.4.W56W43 2010
791.4502'8092—dc22
[B]
2009006339

The illustrations are rendered in acrylic on bristol board.
Book design by Anahid Hamparian
Editor: Margery Cuyler

Printed in Malaysia (T)   First edition   1 3 5 6 4 2

mc Marshall Cavendish
Children

AUTHOR'S NOTE

ONCE UPON A TIME, a poor girl from a Mississippi pig farm talked her way to fame and fortune and came to be a queen. But this is no fairy tale. Oprah Winfrey, the "Queen of Talk," was not born with diamonds in her ears. Even as a little girl, she believed in her own abilities and sensed God's plan for her. Instead of a fairy godmother, Oprah had her grandmother Hattie Mae not only sewing her granddaughter's clothes, but also teaching her reading, writing, arithmetic, and scripture. Smarts would be Oprah's ticket to the ball. Here is the story of how Oprah read at an early age, began speaking in church, and dared to dream of being paid to talk. When she grew up, she became the host of the Emmy Award–winning *Oprah Winfrey Show*, America's most-watched television talk show, and founded Harpo, Inc., a media empire encompassing television and movie productions, magazines, a book club, and radio shows. She received an Oscar nomination for her performance in the film *The Color Purple*. A philanthropist as well as an entertainer, she founded the Oprah Winfrey Leadership Academy, a girls' school in South Africa.

HER DADDY WAS A SOLDIER PASSING THROUGH
and her mother went north to work as a maid.
With a name plucked from the Bible,
little Oprah was left with her grandparents
in a run-down house off a Mississippi dirt road.

God only knew what would become of that child.

No indoor plumbing, just an outhouse,
not even a bed of her own. Sleeping beside
her grandmother, Hattie Mae. Mornings:
emptying the slop jar, drawing well water,
and tending the animals, which Oprah didn't half mind.

The poor farming family barely scraped by
but never went hungry. Grew a garden;
raised pigs, cattle, and chickens; and sold eggs.
"Mama" Hattie Mae sewed every dress Oprah ever wore.
Her only shoes, for Sundays. Weekdays, barefoot.

God guiding her every step.

"Mama" Hattie Mae leaned on the Lord.
"God hears you better when you're on your knees,"
she said. Sundays: church from morning till night.
Oprah watched wasps buzz around the ceiling fan
to the beat of hand clapping and tambourines.

God sure could stir up a crowd.

Every day, Mama Hattie read her Bible.
Read to Oprah, too; taught her reading, writing,
and arithmetic. At three, the child could read alone.
On that farm without so much as a television,
books showed her a wider world, a richer life.

At the same time, her first public speaking—
in church, no less. Little Oprah practiced till she knew
the verse by heart: "Jesus rose on Easter Day.
Hallelujah, hallelujah, all the angels did proclaim!"
And from then on, she was the first child given parts.

God had shone a light on her.

Soon, she was making the rounds at other churches, beaming as grown-ups called her the Little Speaker. Sisters fanned themselves, gushed, "That child is gifted." Mama, proud as could be each time her grandbaby was introduced: "Little Mistress Winfrey."

Surely, God was smiling too.

"Show-off!" other children teased, calling her
Miss Jesus or the Preacher. Some spit on her,
picked fights. She quoted scripture to dodge fists.
When church ladies dropped by,
Mama shushed Oprah and shooed her outdoors.

Mama said, "Children should be seen, not heard."
A tall order for a chatterbox like Oprah.
If she didn't mind her manners, Mama
had a whuppin' in store. "Fetch me a switch,"
she'd say. That was the way back then.

During storms, Mama held Oprah close and said,
"God don't mess with his children." Mama said,
"You gotta do a lot of work in your life and not be afraid.
The strong have got to take care of the others."
Oprah took those words to heart—

learned to lean on God just like Mama did.

With only a corncob doll as a toy and no
playmates, Oprah befriended farm animals,
named them, read to them, and gave them
parts in games and made-up skits.
She even rode bareback on one pig.

First day of kindergarten, Oprah wrote a note
to her teacher. "Dear Miss New,
I do not think I belong here."
The teacher skipped her to first grade.
There, she finally found a friend—Glenda Ray.

God did answer prayers.

When anyone asked Oprah what she'd like to be
when she grew up, she'd say, "I want to be paid to talk."
Back then you could go a month of Sundays
without seeing one black face on TV.
Still, Oprah set her sights high as the heavens—

as if she knew God's plan.

On the back porch, Mama boiled laundry
in a scrub pot that doubled as a bathtub.
One wash day she called Oprah, "Come watch, child;
you'll need to know how to do this someday."
And Oprah said to herself, "No I won't."

Lord knows she was right.